WHEN A GIRL LOVES A HORSE

Margaret Cook
Margaret Cook

PONYBOOKS PLUS INC.

Middlebury, In 46540

WHEN A GIRL LOVES A HORSE

Copyright © April 2020

All Rights Reserved.

All rights reserved. No part of this book may be reproduced in any form or by any electronic or mechanical means including information storage and retrieval systems, without permission in writing from the author. The only exception is by a reviewer, who may quote short excerpts in a review.

This book is a work of fiction. Names, characters, places, and incidents either are products of the author's imagination or are used fictitiously. Any resemblance to actual persons, living or dead, events, or locales is entirely coincidental.

Author: Margaret Cook

Printed in the United States of America

First Printing: May 2020

ISBN- 978-1-7349625-0-5

This book is dedicated to every person who remembers
falling in love with Misty after hearing the story or
reading it themselves when they were children.

And to every woman whose vivid dream,
when she was growing up
was to have her very own pony.

A pony to care for, to ride and to love.

But for reasons known only to the wind,
the sun, moon and stars,
no pony ever appeared in her yard.

WHEN A GIRL LOVES A HORSE

Margaret Cook

Ross Reynolds was a dairy farmer. He and his two Belgian horses, Nellie and Joey Boy worked together, plowing and planting the dark, rich soil and harvesting the bounty of their small family farm.

One day after harnessing the horses to the hay wagon, he lifted his five year old daughter, Anna, and placed her astride Nellie, a gentle mare with a mane the color of honey and a coffee-brown body. Nellie turned her head and tilted her ears toward the girl. "What are you doing on my back?" she seemed to be saying. "Easy, Nellie," Ross said. "It's OK."

To his daughter he said, "Anna, hold onto this." He placed her hand on a short piece of metal on the harness, poking upward, shaped like the horn of a saddle. Ross clucked to the horses. Nellie and Joey Boy took a couple of steps forward. Anna squeezed her knees into Nellie's side. She looked down. The ground seemed to be far away. She smiled to herself. Being in a high place seemed right to her.

Anna saw Nellie's muscles ripple as the mare placed one giant hoof ahead of the other. She held on as her father had shown her. The wagon creaked as it moved slowly across the barnyard down the sunbaked dirt lane toward the hayfield.

"Git up there," Ross commanded. The horses broke into a trot. Anna grasped clusters of Nellie's mane as the ground moved backward beneath her. The friendly warmth of the horse's body filled her with confidence. The girl relaxed and leaned into the rhythm of Nellie's moving hooves. In doing so, she sensed the beginning of something that rarely befalls one so young. Anna knew, without question, she was in a place where she belonged. It was sort of like coming home. "Horses," she decided, "are good."

****

A chilly day in September. Six years old. First day of school. One room. One teacher. Eight grades. Anna Marie Reynolds took her brother's hand and resolutely climbed the five chipped, cracked cement steps that took her into the schoolroom. She wasn't quite sure she wanted to be there today. Ever since that first ride on Nellie, Anna's shadow merged with her father's as he took care of the horses. He showed her how much feed to give them and made a stool for her to use so she could reach their backs as she curried and brushed their coats.

There was something about transforming their shaggy hair into soft, smoothness that gave Anna a sense of peace. She liked to press her cheek against Nellie's neck and close her eyes as she detangled the horse's mane. But this morning there was no time to spend with Nellie. She had to get ready for school.

Anna placed her lunch bucket, containing a peanut butter sandwich, two short celery sticks, an apple and thermos jug of chocolate milk on a shelf in the girl's coatroom. She removed her jacket and stretched her arms upward to hang it on a metal hook. A girl who was taller said, "I'm Carol. Here, let me help. What's your name?"

"Anna."

"Hi Anna. I think you're gonna like school. We have a nice teacher."

The children entered the school area where eight rows of desks stretched the length of the room. In the center was a large, round furnace stove. A blackboard spanned one entire wall. White letters on a green banner above the blackboard displayed the alphabet.

The teacher, Mr. J. D. Weaver, led Anna and the other first graders to the first row of desks. "This is your desk. I expect you to keep it neat and take good care of it," he instructed each child.

When he spoke to Anna, she felt like she should say something to show him she understood. "I will, Mr. Weaver," she promised.

Anna sat quietly and looked around at the other students. They seemed to be waiting for something. The teacher picked up a book and showed it to them. He read the title. *Misty of Chincoteague* written by Marguerite Henry. She leaned forward. "Is he going to read to us?" Anna asked herself. "I hope so!" She always loved to hear her mom or dad read to her and Andrew. She learned that if she let her eyelids fall to meet her lower eyelashes, she could see whatever was happening in the story. Anna looked more closely at the pony on the book cover. "Yes!" She thought. "That must be Misty. And she's looking straight at me."

Mr. Weaver began reading. Anna closed her eyes. The story began with a shipload of ponies escaping from a Spanish Galleon sinking in a wild, unrelenting ocean storm. She saw them struggle to keep their heads above water as waves threatened to push them deep down below the ocean surface. Anna held her breath, willing the ponies to swim. "Please God, please, don't let them drown," She begged silently. When they finally placed hooves on land, she allowed herself to breathe. Her involuntary "OOOOOHHHHHH. Thank you!" could be heard across the schoolroom.

The teacher paused reading, and looked in her direction. "Who was that?" When no one spoke, he said, "I want the child who interrupted this story to stand."

Anna looked at her brother who sat three rows away from the first grade. "What should I do?" her expression seemed to ask.

Andrew raised his hand. "Mr. Weaver, that's my sister. It's her first day here. She doesn't know we're not supposed to talk when you read to us."

The teacher replied. "Thank you Andrew for standing up for your sister. But she must learn to speak for herself."

To Anna he said, "What is your name, child?"

"Anna."

"All right, Anna, I want you to stand and tell us why you spoke when I was reading."

The girl slowly stood, looked at her teacher and placed her hands on her hips. "It was the ponies. I was so happy they didn't drown,"

"Thank you. You may sit down now." He paused, then smiled as he added. "I'm also happy they didn't drown. And tomorrow you'll hear more about what happened to them."

Anna decided she liked school. She looked forward to hearing the stories and poems Mr. Weaver read to them every morning before classwork began. True to his word, he finished the story about the ponies that lived on Assateague Island. She wanted to know more. So she raised her hand and waited to be recognized.

"Yes, Anna," the teacher acknowledged her.

"Is that story true? Was Misty a real pony?"

"People need to decide for themselves whether it's true or not," He told her. "It's one way to explain how the ponies found the island. And yes, Misty is a real pony."

"Is she there now?"

"Yes."

"When I get big, I'm going to go see her."

Anna's teacher caught her seriousness. This was more than a child's wish. It was a statement.

"It wouldn't surprise me if someday you do just that," he said.

****

Anna liked to hear Nellie and Joey-Boy's hooves go clip-clop as they hit the pavement when her father trotted the team down the macadam road that bordered their lawn. Clip Clop. Clip-Clop. She knew she was hearing her father's team, but wondered what kind of sound Misty's hooves made if she were running on a sandy beach. She closed her eyes. Just as she had known would happen, Anna saw a pinto pony trotting by its mother's side.

Anna was learning how to read. But not fast enough for her. "I want to read the book about Misty all by myself," she told Mr. Weaver.

"You will," he assured her.

"But I want to do it NOW."

The teacher took a moment to study the child. "You've learned the letters of the alphabet. And you know the sounds that go with each one of them. If you promise to take good care of it, I'll let you keep the book in your desk and you can try to figure out the words."

"Ohhhh, I promise! I'll take care of it. And then I'll read it to you!"

"I have no doubt about that."

Matching sounds to alphabet letters became a game she could not stop playing. It took longer than she had hoped, but with Mr. Weaver's help, she finally read the first sentence of the story out loud.

He was pleased and somewhat surprised. "Very good, Anna. You are a fine student."

****

December 25, Christmas Morning

Ten year old Andrew Reynold's footprints seemed to appear almost before his boots hit the snowy ground as he raced toward the house. Christmas morning was one day of the year that he didn't like getting up to help his dad milk the cows. He wanted to open Christmas presents before going to the barn, but his parents stood firm. First the chores. Then the gifts.

When he reached the house he swung open the door. Neglecting to stomp the snow off his boots, he left a white trail as he ran through the house and stood at the foot of the stairs. "Mom!" He shouted. "Wake up! Get up! Merry Christmas! Anna, you gotta get up. Now! The cookies you and mom made for Santa Claus are gone. And so are the carrots. I bet he fed them to his reindeer!"

The room held the scent of fresh pine from the tree Andrew and his father had cut and hauled into the house. Long strands of tinsel icicles sparkled on its branches. A garland of popcorn, strung by Anna and their mother contrasted sharply with the green pine needles. Anna looked up at the top of the tree where a large star their mom had cut from cardboard and covered with shiny aluminum foil, had been placed. A string of lights added globs of color among the branches. "Mom, that's so pretty." She said.

The family settled themselves around the tree. Ross handed a long narrow box to his son. "Andrew, this is for you."

The boy slowly opened the package. He stopped when he saw the lettering on the colorful box. "BEN FRANKLIN B-B GUN."

"Dad." The word was laced with delight. "Dad. How did you know this is what I wanted?"

"I was ten years old myself once." His father answered. "I remember what it was like."

Ross reached beneath the tree and picked up another gift. "Anna, this is for you."

"Thank you, daddy." She said.

"You're welcome, Anna, but it's not from mom and me. This is from your teacher, Mr. Weaver," her father explained. "He asked us if it was okay to give it to you. He wrote something in it for you."

Anna detached the ribbon from the package and carefully began to remove the wrapping. "Oh. Oh. Oh," was all she could say when she saw the gift she had been given.

A book. On the cover a pinto pony, standing beside its mother looked at her. Above the horses were the words, MISTY OF CHINCOTEAGUE.

Anna opened the book and saw her teacher's handwriting on the inside cover. "Read it to me, daddy."

She handed the book to her father. He read, "Anna, This was my book. But it is now yours. I look forward to the day when you will read it to me. You are a good student. Merry Christmas. Your teacher, J. D. Weaver.

****

For the next three months, the days of winter rolled slowly across the Reynolds homestead. Anna and her brother liked to pelt their dad with snowballs as he tramped his way to the barn. Ross caught the missiles in his gloved hands and fired them back at the children. "Let's get him!" Andrew yelled as he and Anna charged toward their father. He laughed as he knelt in the snow, completing the ritual by embracing them both.

"Hey kids, let's build the biggest snowman in the county." He challenged them.

"No, daddy." Anna said, "Let's build the biggest snow PONY in the county and name it Misty."

Late in March, winter reluctantly loosened its grip on the land. Anna watched as the April sunbeams of spring melted her snow horse into a tiny puddle of water. "Goodbye

Misty," she said. "But, don't worry. I'll see you someday when I come to Chincoteague."

****

Ross watched his daughter walk across the pasture where Nellie and Joey Boy were grazing. She held a carrot flat in the palm of her hand, as her father had taught her to do. "That way, Nellie won't accidently bite your fingers." He told the girl.

Nellie lowered her head and grasped the offering with her lips. "That tickles!" Anna laughed. She looked back at her father. "Daddy, it looks like Nellie's belly is getting really big. Am I giving her too many carrots?"

"Well Anna, Nellie has a surprise for you. She's going to have a baby."

"Oh daddy. Really?"

"Really."

"When?"

"Any day now."

Anna placed her cheek against the animal's chest and inhaled deeply. The musty sweet smell of horse filled her nostrils. "Can I help take care of it?" she asked her father.

"I'd like that." He said.

"Do you think it will be brown and white like Misty?"

"It probably won't look like your Misty. It's more likely to be the same color as Nellie."

"Oh." Anna's face fell. She considered this. Although she liked the color of Nellie's coat, she also liked the way the patches of brown bounced around each other against a background of white on Misty's body. She wished they could have a spotted horse that looked like Misty.

"Do you think I can ride it?"

Ross heard the pleading in his daughter's voice. "I don't know. You might be too big. What if your feet drag on the ground?" He teased.

Anna changed the subject. "Daddy, when are we going to see Misty?"

It wasn't the first time Ross had heard this question. Although he wanted to take his family on a vacation, the milk checks he received from the dairy didn't stretch far enough to cover the cost of such a trip. Instead of answering her he said, "Come on Anna, help me get the cows in the barn so we can do the milking."

****

J. D. Weaver retired from teaching the same year Anna entered high school. One-room school houses had become a thing of the past when the county consolidated them into one large school campus. His student's families held a farewell party for him. Many adults who had been in his classroom when they were children returned to honor the man who had shepherded and occasionally scolded them through the early years of their education.

The hum of conversation faded into quiet when Joe Stanton, a student from Weaver's first year of teaching, stood and tapped a spoon against a glass. "I propose a toast to this man who dedicated himself to us." He said. "Mr. Weaver, we want you to know we will always remember the stories and poems you read to us. And when we were learning how to read, it seems like you never got tired of hearing us tell Dick and Jane to watch Spot and Puff run. You stood by us when we wrestled with numbers; making them add up, subtract down, multiply and, oh yes, guided us through my personal devil, division. Thank you, sir. Cheers."

As Anna watched people shake hands and exchange farewells with her teacher, she recalled his words from long ago. "I'm also happy that the ponies didn't drown."

"Yes." she told herself. "I'm so lucky that you were my teacher."

****

Anna and the book, <u>Misty of Chincoteague</u>, traveled through time together. High school. College, where she met Robert "Bud" Hadley. "Here, hold this for me." Anna handed him her "Misty" book so she could walk across the stage to receive a Bachelor's Degree in Elementary Education.

Time passed. Life happened. In the years that followed, many words, spoken and read, brought both joy and sadness into Anna's life.

Anna: "I, Anna, take you, Robert, to be my husband, to have and to hold from this day forward, for better or for worse, for richer, for poorer, in sickness and in health, to love and to cherish until death do us part."

Doctor: "Congratulations! You're going to be a mother."

Local Newspaper: "Robert, (Bud) Hadley, killed in action. A hero who saved the lives of 4 men in his platoon in Viet Nam."

Faced with the challenge of raising two children by herself, mixed with her teaching career, Anna postponed her "Misty" dream.

More words.

Daughter: "Mom! You're going to be a grandma!"

Dan Simmons: Anna, I love you. Will you marry me?"

Anna: "I will. But only if you promise me that someday we will walk on the beach where Misty walked."

****

On the first day of the first class she ever taught, Anna had stood before a roomful of third grade children. She picked up a book from her desk, showed them the cover picture, and read the title. "<u>Misty of Chincoteague.</u>" She opened it and began reading. Thirty years later, she read the same book to the last class she taught before retiring.

Misty died in 1972.

Anna and Dan had often talked about the promise Dan made when he asked her to marry him. He knew how Anna yearned to see the place where Misty had been born; how she wanted to see Misty's descendants roll in the sand, trot on the beach, and graze in salt marshes. He knew she wanted to feel the magic that radiated from the beam of the long standing lighthouse as it kept careful watch over the bands of wild ponies. Her excitement when she talked about the ponies was contagious.

Dan caught himself wishing he could see Misty's offspring and the foals that arrived after the pony's time on earth ended. And he knew that if the years could be rolled back,

Anna would have given several of hers to be able to stroke Misty's neck and feel the pony's lips nuzzle her hand. More than once she told him how much she wished she could have caressed the velvety softness of the animal's nose as its warm breath blew on her. Anna didn't want to ride Misty. She only wanted to touch her. Just once. "That's the first place we'll go when you retire." Dan promised her.

****

Anna sat at a table on her sunporch. She took a sip of cinnamon tea and watched a squirrel latch its hind legs on the roof of a bird feeder then stretch down to gobble sunflower seeds. "You rascal." She scolded.

As so often happened, her mind took her back to the night Dan had proposed marriage to her. The smile and surprised look on his face when she told him of the condition upon which she would marry him never failed to delight her. And he had promised. Dan Simmons was a man known for keeping his word. But this time, through no fault of his own, his promise to Anna was destined never to be fulfilled.

"Why did we wait so long?" Anna mused.

This wasn't the first time Anna had searched herself for an answer to that question. The memory of hearing the story of the ponies struggling through a vicious ocean storm to the safety of a sandy beach never abandoned her. She had been so happy they didn't drown. She didn't realize until she entered adulthood that Misty's story proved one thing to her. Bad things do not always come to bring you harm.

"Why **DID** we wait so long?" She asked herself again. Did she secretly want to wait until the perfect time to realize her dream? Was she "saving the best for last" to be shared only with one whom she loved? Or, heaven forbid, what if "the best" turned out to be something very ordinary? What if fulfillment of her dream to visit the land where Misty had lived failed to escort her from the realm of the common into the sanctuary of the sacred? What happens to the dreamer if the dream delivers less than it promises? Is pursuing the dream worth the risk?

"Nonsense," Anna scolded herself. "We waited so long because, because..." Her voice failed. After a long pause, she gathered the courage to speak aloud to herself. "We waited so long because we believed that time would always be there for us."

"There. I've finally been able to say it." Anna continued. There was something about talking to herself that helped her feel settled. "But it's so hard for me to believe that we could have been so, so..." The word for which she was searching would not come to her. Anna sighed.

She leaned across the table to rap on the window in an effort to chase the squirrel off the bird feeder. Her cell phone rang. Anna reached for it, swiped the green "Call" circle on the screen and placed the phone against her ear. "Hello."

"Anna?"

"Carol?" It was her friend, the person who had helped her hang up her coat on a hook that first day of school. Even though Carol was a couple of years older than Anna, the two girls had become close friends. "Oh, Carol, how good to hear your voice. We haven't seen each other for a long time. What's going on?"

"Do you remember our teacher, J. D. Weaver when we were kids?"

"Of course I do. How could any of us forget him?"

"That's what I think too. Did you know he's been admitted to Hospice House?"

"No." Anna winced. "Oh no."

"His daughter told me he has some kind of stage four cancer. I didn't know whether you'd heard about it. "

"Oh Carol. That's so sad." She paused and closed her eyes. "It just isn't fair. He was such a good man. We were so lucky he was our teacher."

"I know. I just knew you'd want to know,"

"Oh, I do," Anna said. She felt moisture pool behind her eyelids. "I'm so glad you told me."

"Good-bye Anna. Take care. Let's get together for lunch next week."

"I'd like that. Good-bye Carol." Anna laid the phone down on the table. As more tears gathered, she knew what she was going to do.

Ninety minutes later, Anna eased her car into a visitor space in a parking lot. She flipped open a mirror on the visor and smoothed down some strands of unruly hair. A book lay on the passenger's seat. Anna took a deep breath then slowly exhaled. This place was stuffed full of memories. It was here that she had sat for hours beside Dan every day for six weeks until he lost his battle with a failing heart. And now, she was going to see another man in her life who was dying. One whom, although she had not realized it, had been her first love. A kind of love only children know. Something pure and innocent, only to be crushed into a thousand pieces as societies' rules about love overrode it.

She walked down a long hallway. She came to room 115 where a small brown sign with gold colored letters announced the resident's name. J. D. Weaver.

Anna gasped. Room 115 was the room where Dan had died. She hesitated. "Why, God?" she wondered. "Why does it have to be this room?"

Anna took a deep breath, then tapped on the door. It was unlatched. It opened slightly from the pressure of her hand. "Mr. Weaver? May I come in?"

A hospital bed held the man in a half-way sitting up position. He turned to look at her. His expression seemed to say. "I should know you."

"I'm Anna. Do you remember me? I'm the little girl who surprised you when I was in second grade. You told me to stand and recite the alphabet and I said it backwards."

He laughed and held his hand toward her as recognition lit up his face. "Anna! I've never forgotten you. Do you still reverse the letters of the alphabet?"

"Z. Y. X," Anna began. They both laughed.

After several minutes of small talk, Anna showed him the book she had carried in with her. "Do you remember giving this to me? It was a Christmas present from you."

He smiled. "Yes, I remember."

"Do you remember what you wrote in it?"

"Yes, I do. And I've been waiting for the day it would happen."

Anna opened the book and began reading. Mr. Weaver touched his hand to hers. She read the first chapter. Not wanting to tire him, she stopped. "Mr. Weaver, I'd like to come back tomorrow and read some more to you."

"I'd like that Anna. Now I'm asking you. Do you remember what you told me you were going to do someday?"

"Do you mean about going to Chincoteague and seeing Misty?"

"Yes. Did you go?"

"No. Misty died."

"You can still go, you know. You won't be able to see or touch her, but something of Misty will be there for you."

Anna thought about this. "I'll come back every day until I've read the whole book to you. Then I'll go to Chincoteague. I'm certain my granddaughter will drive me there."

****

Anna's first glimpse of the ponies was a herd grazing in a salt marsh. She had to adjust her glasses to see them more clearly.

"There they are." She whispered to herself. The animals were so far away they could not possibly have heard her, but she wasn't about to take the chance of startling them. Anna stood for a long time, just looking, drinking in the sight, barely aware of the slight breeze that brushed against her face and left a salty taste on her tongue. Stings from an unruly batch of mosquitoes brought her out of her reverie and sent her diving back into the car.

Later in the day, using a cane to ensure her balance over the uneven sandy beach, Anna made her way over a low dune that ended at the edge of the Atlantic Ocean. The waves rolled forward and back; teasing her toes with its cold wetness. She wandered down the empty beach, farther and farther away from the car. Her granddaughter stayed behind, busy texting and playing games on a cell phone. A horseshoe crab scuttled across the sand, leaving an unusual looking trail behind it. "Look at that! " Anna smiled and said to no one. "Would you just look at that?"

She didn't realize that the waves were coming closer. An extra high wave crashed against the beach, wrapped itself around her ankles and threw her off balance. Anna stumbled and fell to her knees. The wave withdrew. But before she could struggle to her feet, a second one washed around her.

"Help. Somebody help me!" she shouted. "I can't stand up. Help." The wave receded, giving her a brief respite from the force of the water.

Anna was unable to stand, but she could crawl. Crawl she did. The waves kept coming. "Come on hands. Come on knees. We can do this. We can get out of here." she told herself. Placing her right hand ahead of her left, Anna raised her body until her weight rested on hands and knees. She dragged her knees forward. Then raised her left hand, placed it forward and drug her knees ahead. Repeat. Right hand. Drag knees. Left hand. Drag knees. Upon reaching the tide line where the waves did not cross, she flopped down on the sand. Drenched. Exhausted. "Just want to rest for a while. Just want to rest." Anna closed her eyes and allowed the warmth of the sun and gentle rhythm of the ocean to lull her to sleep.

Dusk settled in, transforming the beach into semi-darkness. Anna shivered into wakefulness. Her clothes were damp and cold. But that didn't seem to matter. Her attention was drawn to a pinto pony walking toward her. It moved slowly and deliberately, its hooves delicately touching the ground. The pony was surrounded by a strong, steady light. The animal came closer, watching her, occasionally turning its head to look back, as if it knew it was being followed. Anna sat up and stretched her hand toward the pony. It lowered its head and nuzzled her.

"Misty?" she said. The pony whickered softly. Anna felt its warm breath on her cheek as the pony pressed its head against the woman's chest. "Oh, Misty." The animal moved closer as if to ward away the cold and share its body warmth with her. Anna grasped the pony's neck and pulled herself to her feet. Misty did not move. As the minutes passed. Anna pressed her head against the pony and murmured words she had been saving ever since she was six years old. Words meant to be heard only by Misty. Words that caused Misty to rest her head on Anna's shoulder.

Misty's ears flicked forward. Someone was running toward them. Then a voice. "Grandma! Grandma!" Anna found herself wrapped firmly in her granddaughter's arms. "Oh Grandma, I didn't think I would ever find you. I was going to call for help and then I saw a light moving on the beach. I followed it and it led me to you."

"Honey, I'm all right. But let's not scare the pony. She trotted away when she heard you. But I don't think she went very far. I want to go find her."

"Pony? What pony? There's no pony here."

"Just look at the sand. You can see her hoof prints."

The girl swept the beam of a flashlight across the beach.

"Grandma, I don't see any hoof prints. You must have been dreaming. Come on, we need to get back to the car. We've got to get you warm and dry. We'll turn on the heater and I've got a blanket to put around you. Oh Grandma, I was so scared when I couldn't find you."

Anna knew it was futile to insist that a pony was on the beach. It wasn't the first time that a member of her family had discounted her experience.

"Grandma's really getting old," she heard one of them say when she once overheard them talking.

"She prattles a lot!" another laughed. Anna was not surprised to hear the kids talking about her. She knew that sometimes she talked out loud to herself, often repeated what she had just said and talked about things that lived only in her imagination. But the time had long ago passed when her grandchildren were enchanted by her stories. "Oh, Grandma," they chided her.

When Anna stroked Misty's neck, she had pulled some burrs from the pony's tangled mane. Sharp bristles pricked against her hand. However, Anna knew better than to show them to her granddaughter.

With a sigh and a smile Anna opened her fingers and flung the burrs toward the ocean. She watched a tiny wave pick them up and carry them into the sea. She scanned the area. "Misty couldn't have gone far," Anna thought.

As if agreeing, the moon edged itself from behind a cloud, and shed a soft stream of light across the wet sand. Anna allowed her eyes to follow the yellow-gold trail. There, in the center of a golden pool of moonlight, a pinto pony stood looking at her. It nodded its head, whirled around and galloped away into the darkness.

"Goodbye Misty," Anna whispered. "I know you're here. But no one will ever believe me."

No one, that is, except the moon, the stars, the ocean, and Mr. Weaver.

And, of course, Misty.

Another book from Ponybooks Plus, Inc.

Don't They Just Set You To Dreaming?

Co-authors: Annette Ilowiecki and Margaret Cook

A story-poem that became a song. It retells in poetry form, the legend of how the wild ponies of Chincoteague came to claim Assateague Island as their homeland.

The book is available at shops on Chincoteague, including Sundial Books, Blue Crab Treasures and the Pony Centre.

You can order an autographed pony book directly from us by sending an email to ponybook123@gmail.com.

You can also view pages from the book and private message us on our Facebook page:
Don't They Just Set You To Dreaming?

Use the following link to
hear the song performed by the Three Sheets.

soundcloud.com/3sheets/dont-they-just-set-you-to-dreamin

NOTE: All letters are lower case. The link does not contain an apostrophe in the word,"don't" and there is no "g" on the word, dreamin.

Other books available on Amazon from PONYBOOKD PLUS INC.

Those Who Have Gone Before (Notes from Peg)
A collection of reflections of how our lives are impacted when one among us dies.

Treasure on Boxaurie Mountain
Roger's grandfather relays a family legend to his grandson about a treasure, guarded by an ugly old crone hidden somewhere on nearby Boxaurie Mountain. The boy and his friends make a sacred pact to find and claim it.

Birth of the Catboat
When Andrew Crosby died, it seemed as though his dream of building a boat that could shift easily from deep to shallow water, died with him. But his widow and two sons were determined to turn his dream into reality.

Gullywhomper's Ocean
(E-book) When Jonah ran away from God and was tossed into the sea, he is eaten by Gullywhomper, a very hungry whale.

May you enjoy reading our stories and poems as much as we enjoy writing them.

And now, it's time for us to gallop on into another story.

Peg and Annette

Made in the USA
Middletown, DE
15 November 2022